THE COUNTING BOOK

Judy Hindley

Illustrated by Colin King

Consultant: Betty Root

2 two ✶✶

Two monkeys stole it.

Four rhinos caught it.

Six acrobats picked it up.

Seven crocodiles snapped at the cake.

8 eight ✶✶ ✶✶ ✶✶ ✶✶

Eight firemen saved it.

9 nine ✶✶ ✶✶ ✶✶ ✶✶ ✶

Nine bees buzzed round the cake.

10 ten ★★ ★★ ★★ ★★ ★★

Ten ducks splashed it.

Eleven fish swam under the cake.

12 twelve ✶✶ ✶✶ ✶✶ ✶✶ ✶✶ ✶✶

Twelve frogs jumped over it.

14 fourteen

Fourteen soldiers shot at it.

15 fifteen

Fifteen owls tried to peck the cake.

16 sixteen

Sixteen bears ran to catch it.

17 seventeen

Seventeen squirrels tied up the cake.

18 eighteen

Eighteen mice tried to ride on it.

cake.

20 twenty

Twenty children ate it.

And only the crumbs were left.

1	one	★
2	two	★★
3	three	★★★
4	four	★★★★
5	five	★★★★★
6	six	★★★★★★
7	seven	★★★★★★★
8	eight	★★★★★★★★
9	nine	★★★★★★★★★
10	ten	★★★★★★★★★★
11	eleven	★★★★★★★★★★★
12	twelve	★★★★★★★★★★★★
13	thirteen	★★★★★★★★★★★★★
14	fourteen	★★★★★★★★★★★★★★
15	fifteen	★★★★★★★★★★★★★★★
16	sixteen	★★★★★★★★★★★★★★★★
17	seventeen	★★★★★★★★★★★★★★★★★
18	eighteen	★★★★★★★★★★★★★★★★★★
19	nineteen	★★★★★★★★★★★★★★★★★★★
20	twenty	★★★★★★★★★★★★★★★★★★★★

First published in 1979
by Usborne Publishing Ltd
Usborne House,
83-85 Saffron Hill,
London EC1N 8RT, England
© Usborne Publishing Ltd 1990, 1979
The name Usborne and the device are
Trade Marks of Usborne Publishing Ltd.

Printed in Belgium

All rights reserved. No part of this publication may be reproduced stored in a retrieval system or transmitted in any form or by any means, electronic, mechanical, photocopying, recording or otherwise, without the prior permission of the publisher.